An Umbrella for

Written by
Karen Wiebe

Illustrated by
Katie M. Robertson

An Umbrella for Shay

Printed in Canada

ISBN: 978-1-77069-848-2

Word Alive Press
131 Cordite Road, Winnipeg, MB R3W 1S1
www.wordalivepress.ca

Library and Archives Canada Cataloguing in Publication

Wiebe, Karen, 1955-, author
   An umbrella for Shay / Karen Wiebe.

ISBN 978-1-77069-848-2 (pbk.)

   I. Title.

PS8645.I3228U42 2013   jC813'.6   C2013-903212-6

To: _____

From: _____

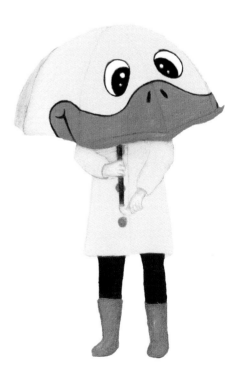

Four-year-old Shay stood on the couch looking out at the gray sky. Raindrops were starting to make little wiggly lines down the window in front of her.

"Mommy, I don't like the rain!" she said.

"Oh?" said Mommy, looking surprised. "There is a reason for the rain, you know!"

"Oh?" said Shay, looking just as surprised.

"Let's go for a walk down to Tuckers' General Store," said Mommy.

Shay agreed, but she didn't smile.

Mommy put on her shiny blue raincoat and her red boots. Shay put on her yellow raincoat and her orange boots.

When they were all ready to go, Mommy smiled at her. "Quack!" she said.

"Quack!" answered Shay, but she didn't smile. People always said "Quack" to Shay when she wore her yellow raincoat and her orange boots. It was fun, and she liked it. Usually it made her smile, but not today.

As they walked along the sidewalk, they saw their neighbor, Mrs. Parker, hurrying to bring her clean laundry in off the clothesline.

"Rain!" she called out to Shay's mommy. "I need to get these things in before they're too wet again!"

"Good idea!" said Mommy.

"Quack!" Mrs. Parker called out to Shay.

"Quack!" answered Shay. But she didn't smile.

"See?" said Mommy. "Rain gives us water to wash our clothes."

"Oh!" said Shay. But she didn't smile.

In the next yard, Mr. and Mrs. Brown sat on their front porch. Their lawn was so green, and the yard was full of beautiful flowers.

"A rain would be so good for the garden!" Mrs. Brown called out to Shay's mommy.

"Your yard is lovely!" said Mommy.

"Quack!" Mr. Brown called out to Shay.

"Quack!" answered Shay. But she didn't smile.

"See?" said Mommy. "Plants need water to grow!"

"Oh!" said Shay. But she didn't smile.

Shay and Mommy stopped to watch some birds drinking from a dish in Mrs. Clarke's yard.

"I love watching the birds!" Mrs. Clarke called out to Shay's mommy.

"Me too!" said Mommy.

"Quack!" Mrs. Clarke called out to Shay.

"Quack!" answered Shay. But she didn't smile.

"See?" said Mommy. "God sends the rain for many good reasons. Everything needs water to live!"

"Oh!" said Shay. But she didn't smile.

When they reached Tuckers' store, Shay was still not happy about the rain, but she was thinking hard about what Mommy had said.

"Good morning!" Mrs. Tucker called out when Shay and Mommy stepped into the store.

"Good morning!" said Shay's mommy.

"Quack!" Mr. Tucker called out to Shay.

"Quack!" answered Shay. But she didn't smile.

As they walked slowly down an aisle of the store, Mommy had an idea. "Popcorn!" she said as she pulled a bag of kernels from the shelf. "Let's have some for a snack when we get home!"

"Okay," agreed Shay. "Umbrellas!" she shouted suddenly as she ran to the other end of the aisle.

Mommy followed her to a rack filled with umbrellas. She pulled out a pretty pink one for Shay to see.

"Would you like this one?" asked Mommy.

"No, thank you," Shay answered politely. But she didn't smile.

Next, Mommy held up a flowery green one. "How about this one?"

"No, thank you," answered Shay. But she didn't smile.

Mommy held up an umbrella that looked like a ladybug. "This one?" asked Mommy.

"No, thank you," answered Shay. But she did smile a little at the ladybug.

They didn't notice Mr. Tucker coming down the aisle behind them.
"Quack!" he said when he reached them, pulling a bright yellow
umbrella from behind his back and handing it to Shay.
"Quack! Quack!" answered Shay, smiling a big happy smile. The
umbrella looked just like a duck!

Mommy chose a blue and red umbrella to match her coat. She paid for their new umbrellas, and they thanked Mr. and Mrs. Tucker.

It was raining much harder when they left the store. Mommy opened up her new blue and red umbrella. Shay opened up her new yellow umbrella. Shay smiled all the way home.

They waved to Mrs. Clarke. "Quack!" called out Mrs. Clarke.

"Quack! Quack!" answered Shay, smiling a big happy smile.

They waved to Mr. And Mrs. Brown. "Quack!" called out Mr. Brown.

"Quack! Quack!" answered Shay, smiling a big happy smile.

They waved to Mrs. Parker. "Quack!" called out Mrs. Parker.

"Quack! Quack!" answered Shay, smiling a big happy smile.

Shay and Mommy danced in the puddles under their new umbrellas.

They peeked out from under their new umbrellas and tasted the

raindrops. It was a good rainy day.

That evening at bedtime, Shay prayed, "Thank You, God, for sending rain. Thank You for grass and flowers and birds! Thank You for puddles! Thank You for Mommy and for my new umbrella! Amen."

And to Mommy she said, "I think I like the rain after all!"

"Oh?" said Mommy. "Me too!"